Copyright © 1995 by Nord-Süd Verlag AG, Gossau Zürich, Switzerland
First published in Switzerland under the title *Valery und König Teddy*
English translation copyright © 1995 by North-South Books Inc.

All rights reserved.
No part of this book may be reproduced or utilized in any form
or by any means, electronic or mechanical, including photocopying,
recording, or any information storage and retrieval system,
without permission in writing from the publisher.

First published in the United States, Great Britain, Canada,
Australia, and New Zealand in 1995 by North-South Books,
an imprint of Nord-Süd Verlag AG, Gossau Zürich, Switzerland.

Distributed in the United States by North-South Books Inc., New York.

Library of Congress Cataloging-in-Publication Data is available.
A CIP catalogue record for this book is available from The British Library.
ISBN 1-55858-447-1 (trade binding)
1 3 5 7 9 TB 10 8 6 4 2
ISBN 1-55858-448-X (library binding)
1 3 5 7 9 LB 10 8 6 4 2
Printed in Belgium

KING TEDDY

Gabriele Kiefer

Illustrated by Jürg Obrist

North-South Books / New York / London

One afternoon, Valerie packed her suitcase and set off to her grandmother's to stay over night for the very first time. On the way, she spotted King Teddy sitting in the grass.

"What are you doing out here?" she asked.

"Waiting for you. Surely you didn't plan to go without me," he said indignantly.

"Why not? If I'm big enough to spend the night at Grandmother's, I don't need a teddy."

"What!" cried Teddy. "Then who will look out for dangerous wolves in the forest around the castle?"

"There are no wolves here," said Valerie. "And no castle, either."

"You can never be sure," Teddy said ominously, and took a careful look around. "After all, you are on your way to Grandmother's, aren't you?"

"Well, yes, but . . ."

"And she *is* ill, isn't she?"

"No, not at all."

"But you're bringing her a basket of goodies . . ."

"No," insisted Valerie. "This is my suitcase. And Grandmother is cooking the dinner."

"Oh," said King Teddy, disappointed. "Well, I'd better come along anyway, just in case. You never know when you may need my protection."

Valerie laughed and took King Teddy's paw in her hand and together they climbed the hill to Grandmother's.

"Look out!" whispered Teddy when they opened the door. "A witch!"

"Silly," said Valerie. "That's my grandmother."

"Ha!" snorted Teddy. "Then why does she have a broom?"

Valerie just shook her head and headed for the kitchen.

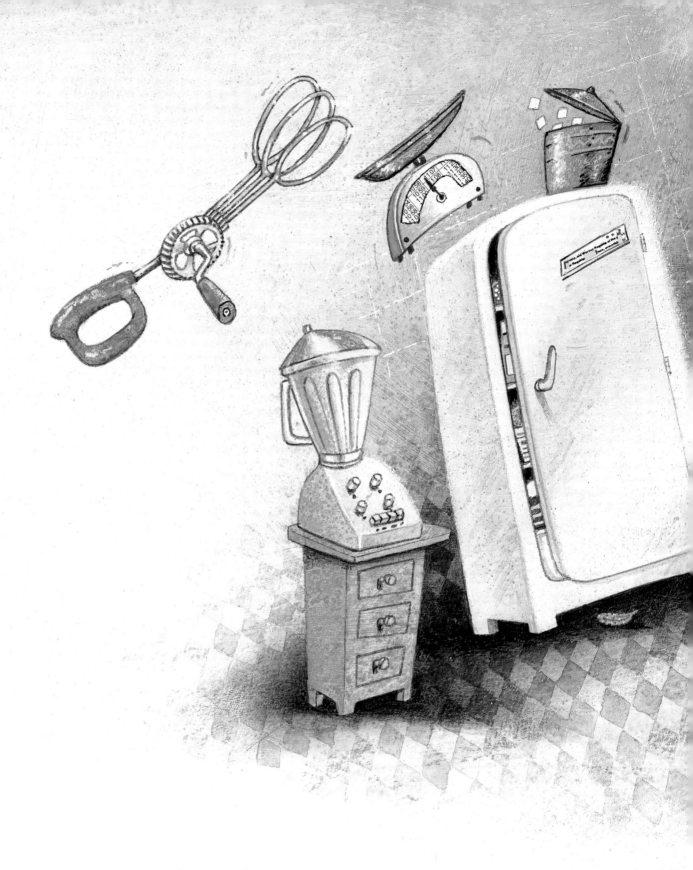

Teddy prowled around, eyeing Grandmother suspiciously. "Don't worry," he told Valerie. "She didn't fool me by moving out of her gingerbread house. We'd better get out of here before she pops us in the oven and cooks us for dinner."

"Oh, Teddy," said Valerie with a smile. "You really are very silly!"

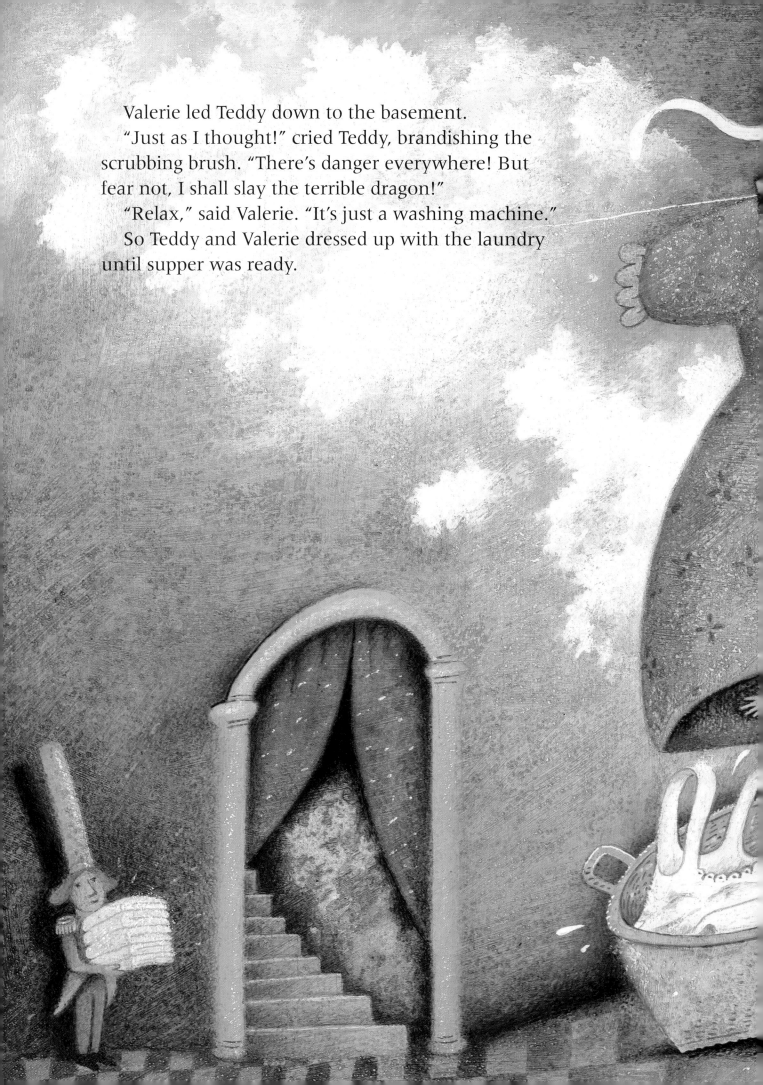

Valerie led Teddy down to the basement.

"Just as I thought!" cried Teddy, brandishing the scrubbing brush. "There's danger everywhere! But fear not, I shall slay the terrible dragon!"

"Relax," said Valerie. "It's just a washing machine."

So Teddy and Valerie dressed up with the laundry until supper was ready.

After supper it was bath time.

"Avast ye, matey!" cried Teddy. "You cannot sail the high seas alone. I'll climb to the crow's nest and shine a beacon to warn bloodthirsty pirates that I'm aboard. If they bother you, I'll make them walk the plank."

Valerie just giggled and playfully splashed water at Teddy.

Then it was time for bed. Grandmother tucked Valerie in and kissed her good night. All of a sudden, Valerie didn't feel so big and brave. The shadows on the walls looked like terrible creatures. "King Teddy?" she whispered. "I'm afraid!"

"There's nothing to fear but fear itself," King Teddy declared from under the bed. "Besides, I'm right here to protect you."

Valerie sighed contentedly, snuggled under the covers, and went to sleep.

Teddy settled down to keep watch, but his eyes grew heavy and soon he was fast asleep and dreaming. He dreamed the dark under Valerie's bed had been transformed into a realm of danger.

Armed and ready, he charged dust mountains
and chased the giant mice lurking behind them.
"Take that, you beasts!" he cried, and with one
sweep vanquished them all.

Valerie slept on peacefully, deep in a dream of her own.
King Teddy had become her giant protector, keeping her
warm and safe all night long.

In the morning, Valerie rewarded King Teddy with a jar of honey. "I guess I'm not as big as I thought," she said. "I'm glad you came with me."

On the way home, Teddy stopped. "I think I'll go and explore a bit," he said. "You are getting bigger and you don't need me around *all* the time. But don't worry, I'll be back by bedtime."

"Good!" said Valerie. "I sleep much better when you're there." Then she hurried home to tell her mother all about her visit to Grandmother's.